The
Dog
That Pitched
a No-Hitter

Also available in paperback

The Dog That Pitched a No-Hitter

Text by Matt Christopher

Illustrated by
Daniel Vasconcellos

Little, Brown and Company
Boston   New York   London

First Paperback Edition

Library of Congress Cataloging-in-Publication Data
Christopher, Matt.
    The dog that pitched a no-hitter / Matt Christopher ; illustrated by Daniel Vasconcellos.
        p.   cm.
    Summary: Mike's telepathic dog Harry is able to send him secret signals about the opposing players on the baseball field, but Mike's weak pitching arm requires them to find another plan to save the game.
    ISBN 0-316-14057-0 (hc) / ISBN 0-316-14103-8 (pb)

    [1. Dogs — Fiction. 2. Extrasensory perception — Fiction. 3. Baseball — Fiction.] I. Vasconcellos, Dan, ill. II. Title.
PZ7.C458Dnp 1988
[E] — dc19   87-16124

11 12 13 14 15 16 17 18 19 20 21 22 23

BIND RITE

Designed by Trisha Hanlon

PRINTED IN THE UNITED STATES OF AMERICA

to Jennifer, Steven, and Philip

The day was hot and muggy, the field was soggy from last night's rain, and Mike didn't feel well. What pitcher would, Mike thought, if he were put into a game in the fifth inning, and his team were trailing by nine runs?

The Lake Avenue Bearcats were beating the Grand Avenue Giants by a score of 19 to 10.

Why do we even have to finish this lousy game? Mike thought. The Bearcats will just pile up more runs against us, that's all.

" 'Cause it's the rules, pal," he heard a voice in his head say. "And you ought to know you can't bend the rules, right?"

Mike glanced over to the Giants' bench and saw Harry, his Airedale, relaxing in the shade. "Right," Mike answered him in his thoughts.

Mike and Harry shared a very special secret: they could communicate with each other through ESP, extrasensory perception. Mike had seen the Airedale in the window of a pet shop one day and was surprised to discover that he could understand the dog's thoughts,

and the dog could understand his! Of course, Mike bought Harry right away, and that was the start of one of the best friendships ever between a kid and a dog.

"This batter's easy," Harry was telling him now. "Keep them down by his knees. He's a sucker for low ones."

"Sure," Mike answered. "If I had good control, I'd try it."

Mike got on the mound, stretched, and threw a pitch. The baseball streaked toward the plate — belt high.

POW! The batter socked it high and deep to center field.

"No sweat," Mike heard Harry say.
"Frankie'll catch it in his back pocket."

Frankie Tuttle, the center fielder, had to run back just a few feet. Maybe he would have been able to catch it in his back pocket if he had tried. But he used his glove instead.

Mike breathed a sigh of relief. One out. Five more to go — two this inning, three the next.

The Bearcats' next batter came to the plate.

"Bugsy O'Toole, Mike," Harry said. "As dangerous as he looks, too."

"I know, I know," said Mike. "He's already got a homer and a triple. Shall I walk him?"

"Keep them low and inside," Harry advised.

Mike aimed at the low inside corner of the plate and for once managed to throw the ball exactly where he wanted it to go. Bugsy O'Toole swung at it, drove a hot grounder to

third base, and Jerry Moon threw him out.

"There you go," said Harry.

Mike smiled. "Thanks, pal," he said.

Harry liked to watch the other teams practice before the games so he could learn the players' strengths and weaknesses. He had a keen eye, but what was really remarkable about him was his memory.

Wish I could remember the way he does, Mike thought.

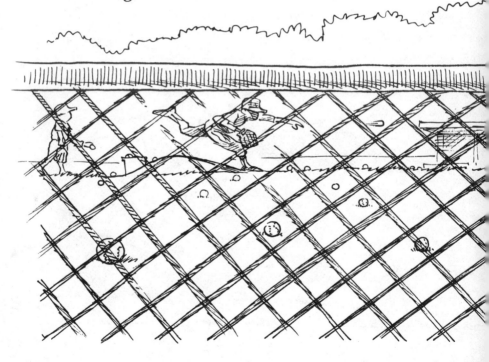

13

The next Bearcat hit a high infield fly. Jim Button, the shortstop, caught it, and the top half of the sixth inning was over.

Mike was relieved for a while, but then the Giants couldn't get a man on base at their turn at bat. Mike was back on the mound before he knew it. He tried hard, but even with the help of Harry's coaching, he allowed two hits, and a man scored. At the top of the seventh, it was Bearcats 20, Giants 10.

The Giants failed to score when they batted for the last time, and the game went to the Bearcats.

TEAM	1	2	3	4	5	6	7	R	H	E
Bearcats	6	1	5	3	4	0	1	20	22	1
Giants	3	0	2	4	1	0		10	14	2

"I shouldn't have let that run score," Mike
said with frustration as he and Harry headed
for home.

"You tried your best. Give yourself some
credit," Harry said. "You sure were better than
that first pitcher."

Mike shrugged. "I hope the coach doesn't decide to have me start against those Peach Street Mudders on Friday. They're no easy pickin's, either."

"I know," said Harry. "They're numero duo."

Mike looked at him. "Numero what?"

Harry grinned. You could always tell he was grinning by the way his mouth curved up at

the corners and the way he lifted his wiry eyebrows.

"Number two," he said. "I've been learning a lot by watching educational television. Like this, for instance."

Harry stopped and did something Mike had never seen him do before: a dance. A crazy dance, on two legs.

"What is *that?*" Mike asked, wide-eyed and laughing.

"You like it?" said Harry. "It's the Bunny Hop."

"You crazy dog! You'd better stop that before some cop picks you up and hikes you to the dog pound!"

"Yeah, right." Harry stopped his crazy dance. "From what I've heard about dog pounds, they're not for an intelligent, capable creature like me."

Mike shook his head. "Harry," he said, "I don't know what to do with you. But I don't know what I'd do without you, either!"

Harry grinned again. Then he hopped up into Mike's arms and licked his face.

The next four days were difficult for Mike.
He worried more about pitching against the
Peach Street Mudders than he did about any
homework or test his teachers could give him.
He'd rather write any report — no matter how
long — than pitch against the Mudders.

The Mudders had played four games so far and won them all. Most of the players were big guys who could hit a ball a country mile. They were players like Barry McGee, who averaged a home run a game, and Turtleneck Jones, who was almost as big and tough as Barry.

"I don't want to think about them," Mike said to himself, while playing catch with his father in the backyard. "Maybe I'll be lucky. Maybe Coach Wilson will have somebody else pitch."

"Pal, you're worrying too much about nothing," said Harry, who was resting comfortably under the shade of a nearby tree. "Relax. Old buddy Harry will tell you what to do. I'll practically pitch the game for you."

"Oh, sure," Mike thought back to Harry, as he caught his father's soft throw. "The great Harry the Airedale. Dog pitcher. Strikes out McGee with the bases loaded. You're out of your mind, Harry."

HARRY THE AIREDALE

"Control, man," said Harry. "All you need is control. I'll tell you what to pitch to each guy as he comes to the plate, and you take it from there."

"That'll be fine, except that I don't have control," Mike grumbled. "All I've got is speed."

"Did you say something, son?" his father asked.

Mike shook his head. "Sorry, Dad," he said. "I was talking to myself."

Sometimes Mike forgot to communicate mentally with Harry and started talking out loud. Mike and Harry had made a pact that nobody — not even Mike's parents — would find out their secret, but sometimes that made for embarrassing moments.

At last came the day of the game against the Peach Street Mudders. And, as Mike had feared, Coach Wilson had him pitch.

The Mudders were first up at bat, and Mike was scared from the start. He walked the first batter and hit the second batter on the foot, putting him on base, too. Then tall, dark-haired Barry McGee strode up to the plate.

"Pitch high and outside to him," said Harry, who by now was pacing back and forth in the Giants' dugout. "That's his weak spot. I watched him during batting practice."

"I'll try," said Mike.

But once again he was too nervous to follow Harry's instructions. He stretched, and pitched. The ball went straight over the heart of the plate. Barry knocked it to center field, where Sparrow Fisher caught it . . . then dropped it!

"Oh, no!" Mike groaned, as he watched two runs score and Barry go safely to second base.

"Have faith, pal," Harry said. "Have faith."

"That's easy for *you* to say," Mike said.

Nobody else scored that inning nor the next. In the third, the Giants got three men on — one on a walk, one on a passed ball by the pitcher, and one on an error, a sizzling ground-er through the third baseman's legs.

Monk Solomon, the Giants' first baseman and only slugger on the team, drilled the first pitch through the pitcher's box to center field. The ball struck something in front of the fielder and bounced over his shoulder to the fence.

By the time the fielder picked it up and threw
it in, all three runners — and Monk — scored.

The Giants' fans went crazy.

It was Grand Avenue Giants, 4; Peach Street
Mudders, 2.

The score stayed that way until the top of the seventh inning, when Mike, nervous as a mouse trapped in a room full of cats, hit the first batter on the shoulder, walked the second, and fumbled the third man's bunt.

"Oh, no!" Mike groaned again. "No outs, and three men on! What'll I do now, Harry?"

A hit could tie the score. A *long* one could put the Mudders ahead. Mike's heart pounded.

"Harry?"

No answer.

Mike looked over to the dugout where he had last seen Harry. But there was no Harry.

Sweat glistened on Mike's face. "Harry!" his mind screamed. "Where are you? I need your moral support . . . now!"

Still no answer.

"Play ball!" cried the ump.

Mike got on the mound. Just then the fans began to laugh.

Mike was flustered. What was so funny? He tried to concentrate on aiming his pitch, but he couldn't remember what the batter usually went for. As the ball left his hand, he knew it was headed right toward the middle

of the plate. He braced himself for the hit that was sure to come.

"Strike!" yelled the ump, to Mike's surprise. The batter must have been distracted, too.

Mike sped another across the plate. "Strike two!"

And another. "Strike three!"

The fans kept roaring with laughter as the next batter — who was trying hard not to laugh, too — stepped up to the plate.

They must be laughing at me, Mike thought. First I fill up the bases, then I get my first strikeout. That *is* something to laugh about.

He struck out the second batter, too.

And the fans kept laughing.

Let 'em laugh, Mike thought to himself. For the first time since the game had started, Mike began to relax.

Then the next batter walked up to the plate. It was Turtleneck Jones. He wasn't laughing. He looked angry and determined.

But Turtleneck tried too hard.

"Strike one!" the ump called, as Turtleneck

swung at Mike's first pitch and missed it by a mile.

"Strike two!" the ump said, as Turtleneck chopped the air a second time.

Then, "Strike three!" the ump yelled, as Turtleneck swished for the third time.

"You did it! You did it!" Monk cried, running to Mike from first base. "You pitched a no-hitter!"

Mike's eyebrows arched. "I did *what?*"

He didn't even realize the game was over until he saw the crowd leaving the grandstand and the fans running toward him, cheering and laughing.

"Nice game, Mike," said Coach Wilson, as he shook Mike's hand. "But I think you got a little help from that dog of yours."

Mike stared at the outfield, where Coach Wilson was pointing. There, doing a crazy, twisting dance on the platform in front of the scoreboard, was Harry.

"Oh, no!" Mike cried. "Is that what the crowd was laughing at?"

"The crowd, and some of the batters, too,"
said the coach. "I think you owe that dog a
few extra dog biscuits tonight, Mike."

Mike grinned. "I sure do!"

Seconds later, Harry came sprinting across
the baseball field toward him.

"Harry!" Mike cried as the dog sprang into
his arms. "What the heck were you doing?"

"The Bunny Hop, remember?" said Harry.
"Want to see me do it again?"

He jumped to the ground and started kick-
ing out his legs.

"I think you've danced enough for one day,"
said Mike, laughing.

When he pulled himself together, he went
on, "Why did you leave me alone out there,
anyway?"

41

"I never left you," said Harry. "I just thought we needed a different strategy. I took some of the pressure off by entertaining the crowd a little."

"Isn't that cheating?"

Harry turned serious. "No way! You pulled your own weight all along. I saw you stand up to Turtleneck Jones."

Mike remembered how relaxed and in control he had felt. "I guess you're right," he admitted.

"Of course I'm right," Harry said. "All you needed was some confidence."

"And a dog who thought he was a rabbit!" Mike said, grinning.

"Naturally," said Harry, who Bunny Hopped all the way home.

42